T0128930

Life and Debt

Life and Debt

(A Rhyme Crime)

Patrick Ryan

iUniverse, Inc.
Bloomington

Life and Debt

iUniverse books may be ordered through booksellers or by contacting:

iUniverse
1663 Liberty Drive
Bloomington, IN 47403
www.iuniverse.com
1-800-Authors (1-800-288-4677)

ISBN: 978-1-4759-8663-1 (sc)
ISBN: 978-1-4759-8677-8 (ebk)

Printed in the United States of America

iUniverse rev. date: 04/13/2013

1.

Mom and Pop sat before the fire
Mom knitted a Christmas sweater while
Pop cleaned out his pipe in ire
There was no small talk about the weather

Mom tried to stay calm, as she rocked back and forth
Pop was miffed with the IRS
They claimed he owed about what he was worth
They'd soon find out if it was worth the stress

Mom was still a petite 58 years old
Her real name was Mary but folks called her Mom
Originally from Albany but now a Brooklyn mold
She had a way about her that made everyone calm

She wore a red Christmas sweater at this time of year
And green pants to round out the colors of the season
The house was decorated to spread the cheer
If this year's spirit were to be different,
  there could only be one reason

Pop was still vibrant at age sixty six
His given name was John Williams but as proprietor of
Pop's shop, he was know simply as Pop
He ran the shoe store since he was twenty six
And for most of this time, felt like he was on top

Pop wore a white shirt, covered with a black sweater
He stood six feet tall and had kept his figure
Retirement thoughts for him were getting stronger
And on this day, 19 December, thought that next year
would see his departure

They gave birth to two children who grew up just fine
Now both in their thirties, they worked with numbers
Both John and Michael had become accountants
Both would be home for Christmas and,
as usual, have all the answers

John and Mary met at Coney Island
It was thirty years ago when they first shared a hot dog
Their relationship was quickened
And to marriage they soon leapfrogged

Mary was a stay at home mom
Mary kept busy until the senior prom
John ran a two person shoe store, full time
John still plied his trade for what seemed like a lifetime

John learned the business, part time, after school
His mentor had come from Italy and wood soon retire
Throughout John's tenure it was always a job for two
For the last ten years John had only one hire

John was always paid as an independent contractor
This meant he was always responsible for his own taxes
John also paid his helpers as self employed cobblers
Including Steve, for the last ten years,
without any catches

But now Steve applied for unemployment
As John was winding down, looking toward retirement
Now the IRS got involved and said
Steve was an employee
And that John owed Steve's taxes for
the last ten years of employment

As mom continued knitting and
John lit his pie before the fire
Both were aware of the IRS meeting tomorrow
Neither spoke as the TV provided background noise
But it wasn't hard to tell that both were annoyed

They bought their house in 1960
After they married, it cost $17,000
It was a three bedroom, colored brightly
Still charming, they improved it as planned

It was a two story house, with a cellar
The coal bin was replaced with oil
Electricity was kept to minimum amperes
And the fireplace often used to keep down the bill

Since the kids moved out, they turned over a bedroom
And then made it into a hobby room
There was still plenty of room for the kids to stay
And all childhood memorabilia was still on display

Tomorrow at nine they had an IRS meeting
So they decided to sleep early tonight
This was no time for idle babbling
They'd wake and face it bushy and bright

2.

It was a crisp 30 degrees on the
morning of December 20
Mom and Pop dressed warmly as they drove to
the IRS office
They decided to act calmly during the inquiry
Blissfully hoping the result would be harmless

Inside the IRS building they spoke to
the woman at the counter
She confirmed their appointment and
directed them to the tower
They were seated in a conference room, which
they found without trouble
And in came a Revenue Officer, acting almost boastful

The Officer wore a white shirt with black pants and tie
His picture ID attached to his belt at the side
Introductions were completed and he sat with a smile
And opened what looked like a good sized file

Mr. Johnson was his name
And he easily pointed out the blame
He said the IRS filed 10 years of returns for the business
And wanted to know how mom and
pop could resolve this

Pop told him he was closing shop at the end of the month
"Doesn't matter", said Johnson because you
owe business and personal both
Pop asked if Mom had any liability
"No", said Johnson, quite reluctantly

"How much do we owe", asked Pop
"With ten years of interest and penalties, it must be a lot"
"You owe over $300,000", said Johnson
"So tell me how you're going to make it lessen"

I'll be on Social Security only, staring next month
I can't get refinanced at my age without any income
I suppose I could pay a couple hundred each month
But any more than that will be a problem

That won't cut it, Johnson scuffed
And by the look on his face, he was about to get rough
I'm recommending we seize you house
And auction it off on the steps of the Courthouse

Mom and Pop looked at each other and gawked
But before they could utter, Johnson continued to talk
We'll be looking at your furniture and car
But even with all this it will only amount to a blip on
your debt radar

Can you really do that, asked Pop, astonished
We've lived our entire lives being honest
And the way you're talking, we'd have nothing to eat

You should have thought about that before
cheating the government
Do you expect Uncle Sam to bear the brunt
I have no sympathy for folks like you
It's my job to make up this revenue

So what do we do, I just told you we'll be living on
Social Security
We can't pay a debt like this so ably
For ten years Steve was paid as a contractor
without a complaint
Because I'm closing shop he applied for unemployment

Again, said Johnson, with attitude
We'll seize your home and garnish your social security
The debt must be paid, you must conclude
If you're ever due a refund, we'll take it firstly

I guess that's that, said Pop
Do what you may, you're the cop
Mom and Pop stood and headed for the door
Another agent entered as they left in an uproar

Mom and Pop vented over their situation
But there was not much they could do
in the way of action
They left the building and got in their car
Today's meeting had indeed been bizarre

Johnson spoke with his colleague and chuckled
I put the fear of God in them, he muffled
Of course we won't take their home
They'll probably pay a couple hundred a month
or get a small loan

I just like using my advantage
Like in the old days before the reform
Back then we could really wage a rampage
But now we're reigned in and have to conform

3.

Early the next morning Mom had the bacon cooking
The aroma of coffee was always alluring
She wondered where Pop was as he was usually punctual
She went to the stairs to call him down, but got no
answer, which made her woeful

Climbing the stairs, she saw the bathroom empty
She opened the bedroom door and screamed
As she saw Pop hanging dead from a beam
There was a piece of paper folded neatly

The note stated he did it to save the family
With him out of the way there was no IRS fee
He apologized for his selfishness
And wished Mom and the kids nothing but the best

Mom called 911 and managed the kitchen
She added some whiskey to her coffee and listened
Her whole life had changed in the blink of an eye
And when she would call the kids, she would not lie

Patrick Ryan

She knew full well who it was that caused this mess
It was none other than the IRS
She swore then and there that she'd get even
Even if it meant her going to prison

4.

Police and other emergency vehicles arrived on the scene
Nothing had been moved or cleaned
As the neighbors peered out their windows
The investigators entered to observe the sorrow

Mom was interviewed in a state of remorse
It was suicide, she stated, in deliberate discourse
Saving the family assets from the IRS was the motive
as she showed Pop's note as being supportive

Pop was handled gently, taken down and
placed on a stretcher
With a blanket covering his body,
he was ready for the coroner
The neighbors were aghast to see the
spread over his head
And all could guess that Pop must be dead

The ambulance sped off and Mom was asked inside
She was told "we don't think you have anything to hide.
We'll check with the IRS on the motive you gave us
And we'll send you a copy of our police report when we
finish our canvas

They finished with their measurements and photos
And expressed their condolences and left her to repose
That's when it hit Mom that she was all alone
And a two in the afternoon, became to bemoan

Although sad at her loss, she was hardened by the reason
And realized her extra assignments this holiday season
she would call her children and let her
neighbors provide comfort
and make arrangements for Pop's final transport

She called her son's, John and Michael
And told them the news, which was awful
She asked them to come home a
day early for the holidays
And when they arrived she provide them with
the full malaise

The neighbors started ringing Mom's doorbell around nine
The brought food, pastries, snacks and wine
None accepted her invitation to come in
They expressed their sorrow and said they'd see her
when the Wake begins

She poured herself some wine and spoke with
the funeral director
He told Mom not to worry and he'd handle all details
without a blunder
They would pick up Pop in the morning for prep
And asked Mom to bring over a nice suit and
shoes for his instep

She went up to bed and slept on her side
Respecting Pop's imaginary space, she gave a sigh
She thought she would never sleep but soon slipped away
And before she knew it the sun woke her at midday

Mom cleaned and dressed, had a bite and left
Taking Pop's personal effects for the final rest
She spent some time at the funeral home
Going over arrangements and then left to roam

She made a few stops to get necessary items
And returned home where she heard Christmas rhythms
Mike and John met her at the door
And helped with the bags as they had always
done before

They opted for drinks before their dinner
To discuss what was must and without much anger
Details explained, they were all quite somber
They tried to stay even but the IRS was abhorred

Mom told her boys she had something important
to tell them
But would like to delay that conversation, she hemmed
The boys agreed and were curious over their repast
But thought it much better not to ask

The next evening at the wake a crowd had gathered
And to Pop's casket they first clamored
All said they were sorry and would be at the funeral
And to the gathering thereafter in the Chapel

The next morning was cold but sunny
Snow flurries swirled in the wind, making it blistery
After a brief church service by Father Runion
They started the funeral procession

At the cemetery, all were dressed warmly
The Williams family given priority
After a few more prayer they lowered Pop's casket
And most dropped in a rose as they passed it

Old friends got caught up at the Chapel
As they ate food, deserts and even apples
Mom and the kids stayed for a couple hours
Then went home, each a little tired

The next day would be Christmas Eve
Normally the time the family would rejoice, not bereave
But they all agreed to carry on as normal
At least to the extent that they were able

At dinner that night the kids asked Mom what she
wanted to tell them
She asked for their patience and said at Christmas
dinner she would give them the details
The kids agreed and went upstairs in the pm
Mom said good night and had a cocktail

At midday on Christmas Eve
They decided on last minute shopping as
a way of reprieve
They spent six hours at the local mall
And drove home through a massive snowfall

As was customary to do on this special day
They started exchanging presents and
there was quite an array
They each had a few drinks and the atmosphere was
jovial
They had some snacks and watched TV on cable

When they retired to bed, the kids wondered
Just what is was that Mom had to offer
They went to sleep a little unsure
But with the knowledge they'd soon have closure

Mom lay awake in bed for awhile
Retracing her plans, which caused her to smile
Tomorrow would be a great Christmas, she thought
And drifted off with very little fraught

5.

It was a very White Christmas with new pure snow
Just like the ones they used to know
They met in the kitchen around ten for breakfast
And no one seemed downcast, by contrast

It was obvious the drive and walkway needed shoveling
Mike and John donned scarf's, hats, boots and gloves
It would take some time and aching
But their appetites would be an octave above

Mom set the dinning room table in Christmas regalia
Everything in the right place, giving it an aura
The colorful clothes and the best china was used
After setting the candles, she stepped back, amused

The smell of Turkey wafted through the air
The side dishes warmed in the best cookware
There were special appetizers prepared
No other day of the year could quite compare

The kids came in and shook off the snow
And alighted from their heavy clothes
Boots were exchanged for slippers
And they admired Mom's Holiday fixtures

Mom suggested drinks and appetizers before dinner
The kids both thought the idea a winner
They sat before the fire and felt warm
Enjoying their beverages in good form

Mom stated that now was the time for their talk
The kids sat back, taking another sip of cognac
"the IRS took something from us", she stated
And I plan to get even, with your help, she ended

I intend to have the IRS pay for Pop's death
The kids listened, almost without taking a breath
We're going to file a thousand tax returns
at a $10,000 refund a clip
And get an obscure attorney to help with
the deposit slips

The kid's jaws dropped at the news
Needless to say, they were confused
Both because the words came from Mom's mouth
And that she wanted to include then both

Mom, they said, you're plan is unusual,
we have concerns
How do you expect to get $10,000 a return
And what makes you think the IRS won't know
And stop you in your tracks with zero

Kids, I know you've both been in the tax biz for years
And have a clientele on computers, that you can steer
I you to find those who always file for an extension
And usually get a refund, anywhere in Manhattan

This way, if we file for them early
The IRS will be unaware until the second claim,
by the real party
That will be four month after the fact
So there should be little or no attention that we'll track

This is where our non-descript lawyer will come in
He'll act as our clearinghouse linchpin
We'll file all returns electronically
And have the refund checks routed to the attorney

Banks usually won't cash an IRS refund for a third party
But an attorney with a client trust account
can do so amply
In other words, we find a lawyer with financial woes
And give him a financial stake so he won't oppose

Then we convert significant funds at a time
Into cashiers checks so we can move them on a dime
The attorney will also get the police report
And file a wrongful death suit at some point

Kids, I know your offices are closed for awhile
But you have access and can begin to compile
The list of taxpayers we can use to file
Transfer them to an e drive disk for our new profile

I need another drink said Mike
Make mine a double, John spiked
Both were reeling already
And needed more alcohol to get steady

Do me a favor asked Mom
Trying to bring some mental balm
You don't need to say anything right now
Sleep on it for a couple of days, now let's have some
Christmas chow

Just a little way into dinner
Mike said, maybe Mom's plan is better
We need to do something for Pop
And the IRS has sent many of my clients to the
pawnshop

John Jr added by saying
I remember a client where the IRS levied his savings
I called the IRS to get a partial levy release
So he could pay rent, utilities and have something to eat

Patrick Ryan

The lady asked me how long since his last meal
And I told her three days before he's had a square deal
She told me it's not a hardship until
he's gone three months without
I called her supervisor and he told me those words never
came out of her mouth

By this time they were enjoying their meal
while intoxicated
And a giggle or tow turned to laughter, unabated
Maybe we can file some returns for celebrities,
John mocked
Yeah, like Sienfeld or Trump, Mike squawked

Christmas dinner turned to fun as the wine flowed
And the three of them played with the idea of
getting a pot of gold
Mike and John told IRS horror stories and laughed
Mom was pleased they'd go forward and sat back

By the time they finally got around to coffee
and Pumpkin Pie
They had discussed some details so the plan
would not go awry
They were still jovial and talkative
All on the same page, furtive and captive

They left the table a mess and had brandy before the fire
And for a moment of so fell silent, as if to admire
They had made a decision they would not turn back
from
And surprisingly or not, they seemed quite calm

The kids inquired about their futures after the deed
Probably the islands in the Caribbean, Mom decreed
John and Mike locked eyes, as if to agree
And strangely enough, they all felt free

Have you searched for our attorney, the kids inquired
Mom said, oh I think I found the perfect esquire
He's been in business for over twenty years
But his career is well behind all his peers

He has a penchant for the horses and boxing
Has lost more that he's gained so we should get his backing
Iv'e made an appointment with him next week
And will wear a neck brace to aid my physique

The kids laughed with their approval
Mom said they should come with her to
make it personal
They all leaned back and took another sip
Thinking of ways they could all help with the flip

6.

The morning sunshine was the queue to awake
Mom was making brunch with eggs and pancakes
John and Mike came downstairs and began to partake
Me and John will go to the office today, said Mike, with
Mom quick on the uptake

They finished their brunch, cleaned and left
And headed for the office, thinking they were deft
Today they would identify the files they needed
for the theft
And put them on portable drives so not to feel bereft

They drove to the office and parked the car
And walked to the office building, which was not so far
They stopped at the desk to sign their names
And told the security officer why they were there, with
little feign

Our Pop passed away a few days ago
So we need to work on his file and set up escrow
I'm sorry to hear that, the officer replied
It's always hard when a loved one dies

Patrick Ryan

They took the elevator to the 37th floor
And used their keys to open the office door
The office was empty as was expected
So they turned on the lights and two computers they
booted

It took six hours but they got what they needed
And closed down the office with the drives in their
pockets
They signed out and left, just as they had intended
And drove back home where they would set up their
templets

They decided to start the project tomorrow
Their excitement was peeked but not so callow
And had drinks by the fire to even the tempo
Mom had dinner almost ready and joined them for
drinks and the narrow

We got our thousand names and more, Mike started
And all from Manhattan, John added
Well that's just great, Mom flattered
So were on our way, she said, as if jaded

The new day brought new activities
For breakfast they had cereal and blueberries
The kids got out their laptops and began their queries
For each client they used a 3 year average for this year's
income entry's

Then they prepared W-2's and other payor information
Like dividends, interest, social security and pensions
After a short break for lunch they went back to work
And by 6 pm, they'd completed the bulwark

They ad cocktails and started a fire
For their daily reports, in the entire
Mike and John Junior assured their Mom
That the returns would be ready for e-file therefrom

They planned on filing about 100 a day
Calculating the refund checks to be received before May
They decided tomorrow they would get PO Boxes
And set in place a forwarding system to receive refunds
in batches

After that they would need to retain their attorney
His name was Robert Olney
He had been studied by Mom, who asked around
And that's how Olney had been found

The Law Office of Robert Olney was located
in Manhattan
In a non-descript building across from Olney's
favorite barman
After Mom gave him the initial pitch
They would invite him to that bar for drinks and
a sandwich

Mom felt sure he would agree to a million dollars in fees
And a condo in the Cayman Islands, with
his own set of keys
From there he could gamble over the internet
And it would all be legal for any amount he could get

7.

Mom gave the kids the locations of the Mail Box etc's
To open accounts and forward to a box central
It would take most of the day to do so
But necessary to make the plan flow

It was a lot of legwork but they got the job done
And each headed home before there was no more sun
They studied their materials before the fire
Had dinner, some television and then retired

The next day brought the last piece of the puzzle
With the Attorney, they'd need to be artful
They had breakfast and left, all eyes twinkled
Hoping it would go down without a wrinkle

When they finally got in to see Attorney Olney
They noticed he had a bit of a belly
He introduced himself and motioned for them to sit,
quite briskly
And asked about their accident and injuries

The office was cluttered with papers and files
everywhere
They wondered how he could navigate his
way around in here
The size of the office was also very cramped
It definitely needed to be revamped

When it was their turn to talk
Mom loosened the Velcro on her neck brace
Attorney Olney gave a small gawk
"oh", he said, another crankcase

Not quite, said Mom, it should be the case of a lifetime
Is a million dollars in your pocket in the next few
months worth your time
This isn't a personal injury case, as you may have
imagined
It has to do with the IRS, glistened

As Olney himself was in trouble with the revenuers
He leaned forward in his chair for further banter
If you're interested in our plan we like
to invite you to lunch
To the bar across the street, for the final punch

They ordered drinks and something to eat
Okay, give it to me, said Olney, and
don't leave out the meat
It's actually a two-pronged attack, said Mom
We want to sue the IRS for wrongful death and create a
financial maelstrom

Mom told Olney about the events leading to their
meeting
She told him of all their planning
Olney listened attentively and continued drinking
About an hour later, he still wasn't withering

Well, that's about it, said Mom, looking at the kids
Do you think we can count you in kind
I've been practicing law for 28 years, said Olney
And you want me to throw it all away, he stated, bristly

Throw what away, Mom asked
You've got nothing in the bank
And you rent an apartment and office flat
Neither of which is worth a tat

With us you could make a million dollars
And be able to decently retire
The alternative is to work till you die
Without even having had much of a life

It'll take you another 20 years to make this kind of
money
And at 66 years old, you can't love what you're doing
that badly
Plus you'll have your own condo right on the beach
You can boat, fish, gamble or even teach

Olney now showed the first sign of a smile
It seemed he was ready to go the extra mile
Okay, I'm interested, how do we start
Mom said, you'll sign us as clients, then do your part

Get our police report and file a complaint
Against the IRS, but don't file it till late
We want it on file for the future
But want to be in the islands before we pursue

Other than that, all you'll basically be doing
Is depositing the checks, until we start moving
We anticipate to have all refunds by mid April
And then convert to cashier's checks, as usual

We'll deposit the cashier's checks in the Islands
Make the checks payable to Tax Group Grand
As we have already filed for a business
name for this entity
And have opened an Island account with a small ante

Start packing for warm weather in early April
And settle your affairs as best you are able
Once we've told you there are no more checks
Empty your account and make tracks

One final thing, said Mom, and that is trust
We won't wrong you and we hope you don't wrong us
Trust is what will hold us together, it's a must
If you break ranks, you'll probably be crushed

We'll all be crushed, blurted Olney, annoyed
What makes you think you also won't be destroyed
Because I have a way, said mom, to avoid the law
And never get tried in court, not at all

That's hard to believe, Olney stammered
Tell me why, the law won't be angered
I'm not saying the authorities won't be mad
Only that my plan is ironclad

What did you think, Mr Olney, that we won't be caught
I'm positive the IRS investigator will find us wrought
Getting caught is all part of the plan
We need to be caught before we can all become a free man

So with that I get back to the issue of trust
You obviously cannot know all of our part of the plan
But if you're willing to go along and hush
I guarantee you'll be a happy and rich man

I haven't had a lunch this interesting in 25 years
When I won the trifecta over a few beers
So, okay, I'm in for the long haul
And at this point, I'd like to thank you for your initial call

8.

Mom and the kids said good-bye to Olney
The were glad that he had agreed
So they drove home somewhat cheery
To discuss matters be fore the fire, frankly

Mom started dinner and Mike made a batch of
Martini's
With frozen glasses and crushed ice, they were a
thing of beauty
Mom joined them in the living room and took a sip
As the nectar went down, she pursed her lips

They discussed their meeting with the attorney
And decided they could trust him, due to the bounty
But they'd keep an eye on him just the same
In case he tried to run some kind of game

The chartered their course and necessary preparation
Mike and John assured Mom all would be ready to start
filing by February
Of course Mom trusted them without caution
And stated all the rest would be timely ready

They ate their dinner never before feeling so close
All on the same page and similarly deposed
To pull off this plan there could be no ego's
Getting in the way and causing woes

As the kids were still on vacation until January
They could work on their prep day by day
By the time New Year's Eve had arrived
The kids had finished their task and sighed

They decided to tie up some loose ends during the day
And to celebrate at home instead of away
They would decorate and make it a Black-Tie affair
And have only the best caviar and stemware

At about 2pm they drove to the delicacy mart
Bought shrimp, filet mignon and lobster too
And went to the checkout with a full cart
They probably wouldn't finish it all this Eve, but they'd
have fun with a redo

Although their spirits were high,
their mindsets were pensive
Not because this special food was so expensive
But as a lie is always an emergency situation
And their recent activities were so alien

Indeed, each felt different, but none would express
That this criminal act had caused some duress
Even though they were hoping for success
They knew great trouble could arise from
building this nest

They were each sure the others felt the same
But tried to suppress it to lessen the pain
They were going against a lifetime of character
And emergencies often lead to the wrong answers

They put their food and beverages in the car
Started home, when John said he wanted a Jaguar
At first Mom and John were startled,
but then laughed out loud
As they could see on John's face that his statement
was made to goad

John had also broken a week's worth of tension
And had momentarily eroded the apprehension
Now they were in the temper of New Year's time
And could enjoy the full evening's pastime

They dressed for the evening and put out the spread
John sang a song or two while playing the guitar
Feelings of good tidings were left unsaid
Until cold lobster was served with a chilled Pinot Noir

John and Mike talked shop while they enjoyed the nosh
Mom was attentive as the talk concerned the IRS
They listened to music on the big box
And for this night they felt quite blessed

As midnight started to near
They turned on the TV to see and hear
Mom went to the kitchen to start the main course
As Mike and John continued to horse

They counted down from ten
And cheered at the year's end
They welcomed in the New Year with a toast
And had midnight dinner with a great host

The repast was fun and very tasty
There was talk of leaving the northern weather,
which was nasty
Even though they knew they should not be hasty
But still, all the same, talked of life on the Islands,
quite bravely

They finished with cups of coffee and cheesecake
And the kids thanked Mom for all she had made
They would retire to slumber until daybreak
And wished each other a great New Year, as if to
persuade

9.

It was back to business for all in January
As usual, the weather was cold and snowy
It was always a let down when the holidays passed
The sun came up late and went down fast

Attorney Olney call and said he got the Police report
And was drafting a complaint to file in court
He said it looked good and there may be a chance
Of at least, what he had gave them a strong stance

Mom asked him not to file it until September
By that time they'd be living in a new manor
And as she predicted the IRS would not
move till October
She didn't want to tip them off any sooner

As both planned to keep their New York addresses in tact
They could still leave in April and not need to come back
They could file the lawsuit and monitor it
over the internet
While they enjoyed the Island weather
and avoid a dragnet

Patrick Ryan

Super Bowl Sunday was just around the corner
t was billed as a game where both teams had good rosters
the game was important for a couple of reasons
the second of which, would see the start of the tax season

The plan was to start filing the Monday after the game
Mike and John had already given their two weeks notice
Better sooner than later, if all just the same
No sense going to work and feel so anxious

So all was in place on the day of the game
They spent most of the day at a ski resort
Utilizing the winter bobsled, on a metal frame
And to keep warn between rides, would have a snort

The Super Bowl finally started at six-thirty
Mostly to give the West Coast a chance to enjoy the day
It was dark in New York and the fire was cozy
The half-time show promised reggae

The game feature the Giants against the Cowboys
And strange as it seemed, the venue was Dallas
Still, they were determined to enjoy
The defeat of the Boys with offensive stasis

The game actually went into overtime
As the Williams family ran out of cheese and wine
Then in the final moment, New York scored
And the local team was quite abhorred

So that was that for football this year
They spoke of where they would watch the next big
game
And reveled in the fact that it would not be here
And the winter sports next year would not be the same

10.

Sitting on the beach, sipping a drink
It had ice and am umbrella that was pink
The weather was warm and the sun was bright
Boy, oh boy, was this the life !!

As Mom and her Son's has assumed
All of the taxpayer's names that they used
Finally filed their own tax returns
Now Mom and her Son's weathered if they'd be burned

Well ir took three years for the IRS to track them down
By that time they had quadrupled their crown
So Mom and her Son's worked out a deal

They gave back the ten million
In exchange for a deal that was written
The IRS would not proceed further
If the trio did not sue the Service for murder
As the Service felt bad about Pop's death
So how Mom and Son's live now is anyone's guess

Anyone's guess

Anyone's guess

But you can be sure they have nothing but the best

Nothing but the best

The moral of the story is simple

Be true and straight with other people

Be true and straight with other people

The End

Printed in the United States
By Bookmasters